The Detective of London

by Robert Kraus and Bruce Kraus

illustrated by Robert Byrd

Windmill Books and E. P. Dutton / New York

For Pamela and Billy
R.K.

For Margie
B.K.

For Rob and Jennifer
R.B.

Text copyright © by Robert Kraus and Bruce Kraus   1977
Illustrations copyright © by Robert Byrd   1977
Published by Windmill Books & E. P. Dutton
201 Park Avenue South, New York, New York 10003

Library of Congress Cataloging in Publication Data
Kraus, Robert, The Detective of London.
[1. Mystery and detective stories]
I. Kraus, Bruce, joint author.
II. Byrd, Robert.   III. Title.
PZ7.K868De   [E]   77-24450
ISBN 0-525-61568-7

Published simultaneously in Canada by Clarke, Irwin,
& Company, Limited, Toronto and Vancouver

Typography by The Composing Room
Designed by Ann Gold
Edited by Robert Kraus

Printed in the U.S.A.   First Edition
10 9 8 7 6 5 4 3 2 1

Professor Herringbone had spent years battling the winds of the Gobi Desert, unearthing the bones of dinosaurs.

He loaded them on the great research ship of the London Scientific Society and set sail for England.

The bones were to be the showpiece of Queen Victoria's Diamond Jubilee Celebration.

The crowned heads of Europe were all on their way to pay their respects to the Queen and to view the Professor's great discoveries.

But the day before the opening of the celebration, the bones mysteriously disappeared from the London docks.

The Prime Minister, the Lord Chancellor, the Director of the British Museum and Scotland Yard were totally baffled by the case. They all turned to me.

I am the Detective of London.

Disguised as a sailor of the merchant marine, I searched
the docks of London for clues. But I found no clues. I
found no bones. I did, however, find some barrels
which contained kippered herring and had a tasty
snack.

I questioned an informant on the London Bridge. He couldn't advise me about the bones, but he did recommend a good tea shop in Piccadilly Circus.

In Piccadilly Circus, I had a spot of tea and some cucumber sandwiches. But I saw no sign of the missing bones.

At Trafalgar Square, crime in the streets was flourishing, but the criminals had never heard of dinosaur bones.

I did have a tasty snack of fish and chips, while consid-
ering the facts.

I paid a visit to Professor Herringbone of the British Museum, who was most eager for news of the case.

"Do tell, what have you discovered so far?" he asked.

"First of all, there was no sign of the bones on the London docks."

"That's too bad."

"Indeed it is not. It shows that the thief appreciated the bones' true value and is keeping them safe."

"Second," I continued, "the bones are not offered for sale on the Black Market."

"So you've wasted your time, no?"

"On the contrary, it means that the thief wanted the bones for his own use, not to sell. And who, Professor, would have any use for dinosaur bones?"

"A dinosaur?" asked the professor.

"A professional scientist," I replied.

"But," said Professor Herringbone, "all the scientists in England belong to the Scientific Society which sponsored my expedition and can study the bones any time they wish. So it couldn't be one of them," he insisted.

"Precisely," I replied, "the thief therefore could only have been a scientist expelled from the Society and one with a passionate interest in bones. Can you think of such a one, Professor?"

"Why of course! I should have thought of it myself. Last year the Society expelled a Dr. S. S. Beagle. He had some odd theory that dogs are all descended from wolves. Everyone in the Society laughed at him. He still has a laboratory at Oxford, I think."

"Thank you, Professor. I'm on my way."

I ran to catch the next train to Oxford, snacking on a
crumpet with orange marmalade on the way.

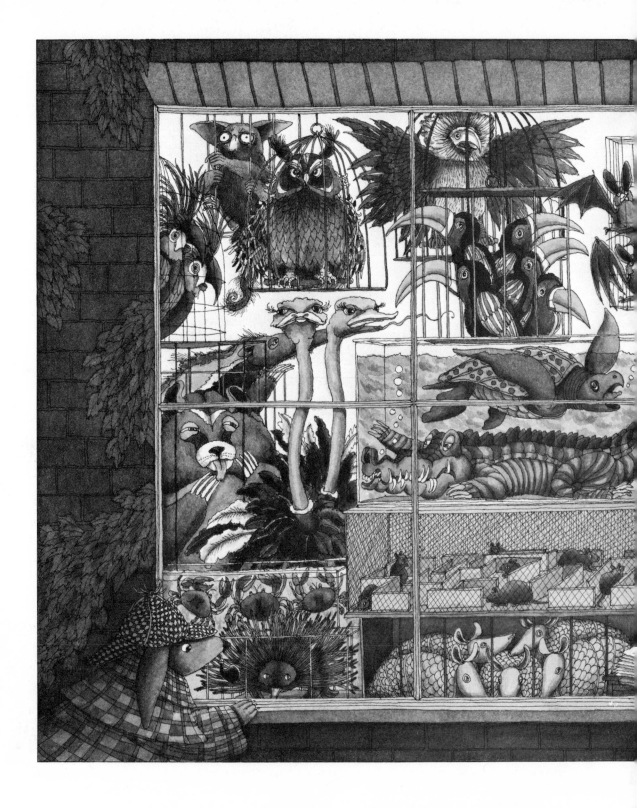

I arrived to discover Dr. Beagle at work in his laboratory amid hundreds of caged animals and birds.

"Dr. Beagle, I presume!"

"The Detective of London!" exclaimed Beagle. "Only you could have found me out. Laughed out of the Society, I had to steal the bones to prove my theory."

"I understand, Doctor, but we must get these bones to London, for the Queen's Jubilee is about to begin."

"But you can't," he exclaimed, "my work must continue! My theories will reshape the world!"

"Patience, Doctor, your theory will have its day. But first, justice must be done, and I believe that the Queen's judges will lighten your sentence if you cooperate with us now."

Now that the fear of Newgate Prison was in him, he quickly hit upon a plan. He lead me to a low seaman's dive on the waterfront where a captain's crew could be recruited to return the bones to London.

The recruiting was simple but efficient. "You can't
make an omelette without cracking eggs," said Dr.
Beagle.

The motley crew worked through the night. We
loaded the cargo and were off to our destination.

When we dropped anchor, the banks of the Thames were lined with cheering crowds and visiting dignitaries from the world over. Our mission was accomplished and just in the nick of time.

"You've saved the day," exclaimed the Prime Minister, warmly shaking my hand. "You're a hero, a miracle worker!"

"Not at all," I replied. "I am simply the Detective of London."